Dragons
& Mythical Beasts

Dragons
& Mythical Beasts
A CELEBRATION OF LEGENDARY CREATURES

Alastair Horne

First published in 2025

Copyright © 2025 Amber Books Ltd

All rights reserved. No part of this publication may be reproduced, stored in a retrieval system, or transmitted in any form or by any means, electronic, mechanical, photocopying, recording, or otherwise, without prior written permission of the copyright holder.

Published by
Amber Books Ltd
United House
London N7 9DP
United Kingdom
www.amberbooks.co.uk
Facebook: amberbooks
YouTube: amberbooksltd
Instagram: amberbooksltd
X(Twitter): @amberbooks

ISBN: 978-1-83886-600-6

Project Editor: Anna Brownbridge
Designer: Keren Harragan
Picture Research: Terry Forshaw

Printed in China

Contents

Introduction	6	**Dragons from Literature**	
		Beowulf and the Dragon	90
Dragons from Folklore		Smaug	92
St. George and the Dragon	10	Glaurung	91
Beithir	12	Drogon, Rhaegal, and Viserion	96
The dragons of Dinas Emrys	14	Hungarian Horntail	98
Lambton Worm	16	Norwegian Ridgeback	100
The Lyminster Knucker	18	Swedish Short-Snout	102
The Bisterne Dragon	20	Kalessin	104
Cockatrice	22	The dragons of Pern	106
Peluda	24		
Tarasque	26	**Mythical Creatures from Legends**	
Cadmus and the Ismenian dragon	28	Sphinx	110
The Hydra	30	Phoenix	112
The Dragon of Colchis	32	Cerberus	114
Ladon	34	Chimera	116
Balaur	36	Pegasus	118
Sárkány	38	Centaur	120
Lagarfljót Worm	40	Scylla and Charybdis	122
Fáfnir	42	The Cyclopes	124
The Wawel Dragon	44	Gorgons	126
Kulshedra	46	Griffin	128
Leviathan	48	Harpy	130
Mušḫuššu	50	Minotaur	132
Bahram Gur and the dragon	52	Unicorn	134
Zilant	54	Faun	136
Apep	56	Kelpie	138
Ouroboros	58	Selkie	140
Ninki Nanka	60	Dwarf	142
Nyami Nyami	62	Elf	144
Ryūjin	64	Vampire	146
Wani	66	Jörmungandr	148
Zennyo Ryūō	68	Vritra	150
Kuzuryū	70	Makara	152
Ao Guang	72	Manticore	154
Dragon turtle	74	Mermaid	156
Shenlong	76	Golem	158
Gaasyendietha	78		
Horned serpent	80	Picture Credits	160
Amaru	82		
Bakunawa	84		
Poubi Lai	86		

Introduction

People have always told stories, no matter where – or when – they are. And throughout history, many of those stories have concerned strange, almost unbelievable creatures. The dragons and mythical beasts whose stories you'll find in this book range from the highlands of Scotland to the depths of Lake Ontario, from near-prehistoric Mesopotamia to medieval China, and from ancient Greece to the twenty-first century swamps of West Africa.

These stories stretch through time. Mythical monsters from past

millennia, invented to explain the creation of the world, or natural phenomena such as earthquakes and droughts, are reimagined for new times, new audiences, and new media; they take flight into books, films, and video games, updated to fit our own particular needs. In the novels of Anne McCaffrey, for instance, the dragons of Pern are not magical creatures but a genetically engineered alien race, while vampires – in the form of *Twilight's* Edward Cullen and *Buffy's* Angel – have become romantic figures loved by heroines … and by a large proportion of their audience!

In the pages that follow, you'll encounter many familiar faces – several, no doubt, breathing fire! But I hope you'll also find plenty more that are new to you, from unfamiliar cultures and times, that will surprise, delight, and maybe even astonish.

Dragons from Folklore

You might think you could immediately recognise a dragon; that its wings, horns, and fiery breath would easily give it away. But dragons are very varied, and there are no scientific definitions or taxonomies to say precisely what they are. And so, among the dragons here you'll find not only Smaug from *The Hobbit* and the dragon slain by Saint George, but also sea serpents, wyrms, dragons with multiple heads, and – perhaps most frightening of all – shapeshifting dragons that take human form.

Jason killing the Colchian Dragon *by Christian Wilhelm Ernst Dietrich, c. 1766–1770.*

St. George and the Dragon

According to legend, St. George was a knight who rescued a Libyan princess from certain death by slaying the dragon that demanded daily tribute from local villagers. When early offerings of jewels and animals had failed to satisfy the dragon's greed, human sacrifices had been required, and the princess was to be his latest victim. George has been the patron saint of England since the reign of King Edward III in the fourteenth century.

Once upon a time...
Before his name became associated with dragons, St. George is originally believed to have been a Roman soldier executed by the Emperor Diocletian in the fourth century AD for refusing to renounce his Christian faith.

Origins:
It was not until around the eleventh century that George began to be associated with a dragon.

In popular culture:
Depictions of St. George slaying the dragon can be found in works of art across Europe and Africa, and on three different English bank notes, from 1917 to 1993.

Raphael's painting *St. George and the Dragon*, c. 1505,
can be found in the Louvre in Paris.

*"There were many English knights that Pagans did convert.
But St. George, St. George pluckt out the dragon's heart."*

– *Traditional English ballad*

"A serpent, whenever encountered, ought to be killed. Otherwise, the encounter will prove an omen of evil."

– John Gregerson Campbell,
Superstitions of the Highlands and Islands of Scotland

In Welsh mythology, white dragons are associated with Anglo-Saxons.

Beithir

ne of the many monsters associated with water in Scottish folklore, the dragon-like Beithir may lack the wings or fiery breath typically associated with dragons, but they are said to possess a venomous sting that kills its victims unless they can reach a river or loch before the beast itself does. Living in mountain caves or valleys, the Beithir's name – which derives from Scottish Gaelic – is thought to mean 'wild beast', 'thunderbolt', or 'serpent'.

Once upon a time…
A Beithir on the Scottish isle of Islay was said to have consumed seven horses before being lured into a loch and onto a line of barrels filled with spikes and explosives.

Origins:
Beithir are thought to be born from dead serpents; only separating the head from the body and then destroying it will prevent the carcass from taking on its new form.

In popular culture:
Beithir appear in the *Dungeons and Dragons Monster Manual*, where they are described as 'a combination of centipede and crocodile'.

The dragons of Dinas Emrys

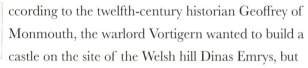ccording to the twelfth-century historian Geoffrey of Monmouth, the warlord Vortigern wanted to build a castle on the site of the Welsh hill Dinas Emrys, but each night the stonework collapsed. A mysterious young boy was chosen as a sacrifice to remove any curse, but he explained that two dragons were fighting in a pool beneath the hill, shaking the foundations to the ground. The castle could not be built until the red dragon had defeated the white.

Once upon a time...
The young boy who gave Vortigern this advice was called Myrddin Emrys; he would later take the name Merlin and become the wizard in the legends of King Arthur.

Origins:
The two dragons had reportedly been buried at Dinas Emrys by the mythical Welsh hero Lludd Llaw Eraint.

In popular culture:
The victorious red dragon has served as the national animal of Wales for more than fourteen centuries and features prominently on the Welsh flag.

The red and white dragons fought each other near the Welsh hill Dinas Emrys.

"The red serpent is your dragon, but the white serpent is the dragon of the people who occupy several provinces and districts of Britain."

– *Nennius's* The History of the Britons

The Knight John Lambton strikes the monster with his sword.

*"This feorful worm wad often feed
On calves an' lambs an' sheep
An' swally little bairns alive
When they laid doon to sleep."*

– *Clarence M. Leumane*, The Lambton Worm

Lambton Worm

he legend of the Lambton Worm – 'worm' being an Old English word for 'serpent' or 'dragon' – comes from County Durham. Large enough to wrap itself seven times around a local hill, the Lambton Worm terrorised villagers, devouring animals and children, before it was killed by John Lambton, a knight returning from the crusades, with the help of a local white witch. The witch warned Lambton that his family would be cursed unless he killed the first living thing he saw after he defeated the worm.

Once upon a time…
To avoid the curse, Lambton's father was instructed to release his son's favourite hound to greet him – and be killed – but he forgot.

Origins:
The worm was originally caught by Lambton as a child when skipping church to fish one Sunday morning. He dropped it into a well, where it later grew to its full size.

In popular culture:
The Lair of the White Worm, a 1911 novel by Bram Stoker, the author of *Dracula*, is heavily influenced by the legend of the Lambton Worm.

The Lyminster Knucker

egend has it that the people of the Sussex village of Lyminster were terrorised by a type of water dragon native to the county, known locally as a Knucker. When the King of Sussex's daughter was threatened by this terrible beast, he offered her hand in marriage to whoever could rescue her. A wandering knight accepted the challenge and dispatched the dragon; a stone in Lyminster churchyard, the Slayer's Slab, is thought to mark his grave.

Once upon a time…
According to a different version of the legend, the Knucker was killed by a farmer's boy who fed it an enormous poisoned pie. The dragon ate not only the pie but also the horse and cart that delivered it.

Origins:
Knuckers were believed to occupy bottomless pools of water known as 'knuckerholes'. The Lyminster Knuckerhole was just north of the village.

In popular culture:
In *Sláine*, a comic-book adventure by Pat Mills from 2000 AD, the eponymous hero rides an ageing dragon called The Knucker.

Stained glass windows at Lyminster depict the slaying of the Knucker.

"Perhaps all the dragons of our lives are princesses who are only waiting to see us once beautiful and brave."

–Rainer Maria Rilke, Letters to a Young Poet

The Bisterne Dragon

oltons Bench, a hill outside the village of Lyndhurst in Hampshire, is believed to be the final resting place of the Bisterne Dragon, which forced the villagers of nearby Bisterne to supply it every morning with a tribute of fresh milk. It was slain by the knight Sir Maurice Berkeley, who hid in a hut with his dogs until the dragon arrived one morning, having covered his armour with glass to protect himself from its attack.

Once upon a time...
Berkeley may have defeated the dragon, but only at great personal cost: he died 30 days later and was buried atop Boltons Bench, his yew-wood bow living on in the shape of the yew tree that still stands on the hill.

Origins:
A scroll at Berkeley Castle in Gloucestershire tells the tale of how the dragon was slain by the lord of the manor, 'Sir Moris Barkley'.

In popular culture:
Several inns around Bisterne are named 'the Green Dragon' in honour of the myth.

A knight, attended by his dogs, is surprised by a dragon in the woods.

"So comes snow after fire, and even dragons have their ending!"

– *J.R.R. Tolkien,* The Hobbit

"Hath Romeo slain himself? Say thou but 'Ay,'
And that bare vowel 'I' shall poison more
Than the death-darting eye of cockatrice."

– *William Shakespeare*, Romeo and Juliet

A cockatrice extends its triangular-pointed tongue.

Cockatrice

A two-legged dragon with the head of a rooster, a cockatrice was believed to be born when a cockerel's egg was hatched by a snake or toad. It could kill people merely by touching them, looking at them, or breathing on them, and could only be killed itself by being shown its own reflection in a mirror, or by hearing the crow of a cockerel. The only creature thought immune to its death-dealing glance was the weasel.

Once upon a time...
In the Swiss city of Basel in 1474, a cockerel was accused of laying a cockatrice egg; it was put on trial and sentenced to death.

Origins:
The first use of the word 'cockatrice' in English occurs in John Wycliffe's fourteenth-century translation of the Bible.

In popular culture:
In *Harry Potter and the Goblet of Fire*, Hermione Granger explains that a cockatrice caused the cancellation of the Triwizard Tournaments for two hundred years by escaping and attacking three headmasters.

Peluda

he Peluda – known in English as 'the Hairy Beast of La Ferté-Bernard' – was a dragon-like creature with the head and tail of a serpent and an egg-shaped body whose long green fur hid sharp stinging spikes like those of a porcupine. It lived on the banks of the River Huisne, not far from the French city of La Ferté-Bernard, destroying crops and killing animals and people, before being killed by a blow to its tail from the fiancé of a maiden it had threatened.

Once upon a time...
When the Peluda retreated into the River Huisne to shelter from the citizens of La Ferté-Bernard', it flooded the surrounding fields, destroying crops and causing a famine.

Origins:
The Peluda was thought to date back to Old Testament times, surviving the flood despite being forbidden by Noah from coming on the ark.

In popular culture:
The Peluda features in *The Book of Imaginary Beings* by Argentinian writer Jorge Luis Borges, an anthology of mythical creatures.

*"She hurried at his words, beset with fears,
For there were sleeping dragons all around."*

– Robert Keats, 'The Eve of St. Agnes'

The Peluda had distinctive green fur, sharp spikes, and a long tail.

25

"There was that time a great dragon, half beast and half fish, greater than an ox, longer than a horse, having teeth sharp as a sword, and horned on either side."

– *Jacobus de Voragine,* The Golden Legend

This sculpture of the Tarasque stands outside the Château de Tarascon, France.

Tarasque

 nlike the many dragons slain by heroic knights and fearsome warriors, the Tarasque – a dragon described as being half animal and half fish, with sword-like teeth – is said to have been defeated by Saint Martha, one of the sisters of Lazarus raised from the dead in the Bible. She calmed the beast with holy water before tying it up so that villagers it had threatened – in Provence in France – could kill it with rocks and spears.

Once upon a time...
The story of Saint Martha and the Tarasque features in Jacobus de Voragine's collection of saints' lives, *The Golden Legend*.

Origins:
The Tarasque was thought to be a cross between Leviathan from the Bible and a Galatian creature called Onachus whose caustic dung caused burns to those it touched.

In popular culture:
A sculpture of the Tarasque can be found outside the Château de Tarascon in the South of France, and a festival is held each year in Tarascon in June.

Cadmus and the Ismenian Dragon

ccording to Greek myth, the Ismenian Dragon was the son of the god Ares, whose sacred spring in Boeotia he guarded fiercely. When Cadmus, a prince of Phoenicia, sent his followers to the spring to get water for a sacrifice to the goddess Athena, the dragon killed them. Cadmus avenged their deaths by killing the dragon but, as a punishment for killing Ares's son, was forced to serve the god for the next eight years.

Once upon a time...
On the instructions of the goddess Athena, Cadmus sowed the dragon's teeth into the nearby fields. A hundred armoured warriors sprang up and fought among themselves until only five were left.

Origins:
Cadmus had originally begun his expedition in search of his sister Europa, who had been carried off to Crete by Zeus, king of the gods, while in the shape of a bull.

In popular culture:
In E. Nesbit's novel *The Wouldbegoods*, the Bastable children sow what they think are dragons' teeth only to discover a troop of soldiers on the site the next day.

Cadmus slays the Ismenian dragon with his spear.

*"We did sow those dragon's teeth
in Randall's ten-acre meadow,
and what do you think has come up? …
a camp of soldiers."*

– *E. Nesbit*, The Wouldbegoods

"As each of its hundred heads was cut away, another grew in its place."

– *Ovid*, Metamorphoses

Hercules could not defeat the hydra without the assistance of his nephew.

The Hydra

n Greek and Roman mythology, the hydra was a ferocious serpentine monster with poisonous breath; whenever one of its many heads was cut off, it grew two more from the stump. Killing the hydra was the second of the labours of Hercules, who was only able to defeat the creature with the help of his nephew Iolaus. Each time Hercules cut off a head, Iolaus burned the stump with a firebrand to prevent new heads from growing.

Once upon a time…
After the hydra was killed, the goddess Hera placed it in the night sky as a constellation.

Origins:
Hera had deliberately placed the hydra at Lake Lerna, an entrance to the Underworld, in one of her many attempts to kill her hated stepson Hercules.

In popular culture:
In Marvel comics, the villainous organisation Hydra takes not only its name but also its motto from the mythical creature: 'If a head is cut off, two more shall take its place'.

The Dragon of Colchis

When Jason and his argonauts arrived in Colchis to claim the golden fleece, he was given three tasks to accomplish by its owner, King Aeetes. The last of these was to defeat the serpentine dragon that guarded the fleece, which famously never slept. Aeetes's daughter Medea, who had fallen in love with Jason, gave him a potion which put the dragon to sleep, and the pair escaped with their treasure.

Once upon a time...
Jason's second task had been – like Hercules – to sow a dragon's teeth into a field and to defeat the soldiers that grew from the ground as a result.

Origins:
Like the hydra and Cerberus, the triple-headed dog guarding the entrance to the underworld, the Colchian dragon was thought to be the offspring of the giant Typhon and Echidna, a monstrous creature, part-snake and part-woman.

In popular culture:
Jason's search for the golden fleece features in the 1963 film *Jason and the Argonauts*, famous for Ray Harryhausen's stop-motion animation.

While the Colchian dragon is distracted, Jason steals the golden fleece.

*"While that great monster slept,
the hero took the Golden Fleece;
and proudly sailed away
bearing his treasure."*

– *Ovid*, Metamorphoses

"Slain by Hercules, he lay fallen by the trunk of the apple-tree; only the tip of his tail was still writhing."

– *Apollonius Rhodius,* The Argonautica

Hercules draws his bow against the dragon Ladon.

Ladon

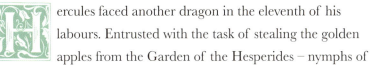

ercules faced another dragon in the eleventh of his labours. Entrusted with the task of stealing the golden apples from the Garden of the Hesperides – nymphs of sunset and evenings – the hero shot the dragon Ladon, the apples' guardian, with a bow and arrow before taking the fruit. (Another version of the story has Hercules tricking the Titan Atlas into stealing the apples on his behalf.)

Once upon a time...
Jason and his Argonauts saw Ladon's corpse the following day when they passed by the Garden of the Hesperides on their way home with the golden fleece.

Origins:
According to Apollodorus, Ladon was another of the offspring of Typhon and Echidna, though other sources suggest he was the son of the sea gods Phorcys and Ceto.

In popular culture:
The Labours of Hercules, a 1947 collection of short stories by Agatha Christie, features her Belgian detective Hercule Poirot undertaking cases echoing the myths.

Balaur

he Romanian Balaur are enormous many-headed dragons famous for guarding hoards of treasure and abducting virtuous young women. Some inhabit wells, where they demand the sacrifice of maidens; others are to be found in Armenia and can produce precious stones from their saliva. A third type is airborne, causing strange weather whenever it encounters – and fights with – another of its species.

Once upon a time...
Romanian folktales often feature Balaur who have captured princesses – often called Ileana Cosânzeana ('the embodiment of feminine beauty') – and are slain by a hero known as Făt-Frumos ('the handsome lad').

Origins:
According to some legends, the dragons ridden by the Solomonari – Romanian wizards who control the weather – are Balaur.

In popular culture:
The online role-playing game Aion features a race of dragons called the Balaur.

When Balaur dragons fight each other, strange weather ensues.

 *"A dragon without its rider is a tragedy. A rider without their dragon is dead."*

– *Rebecca Yarros*, Fourth Wing

*"The brave men did not kill dragons.
The brave men rode them."*

– Viserys Targaryen in Game of Thrones

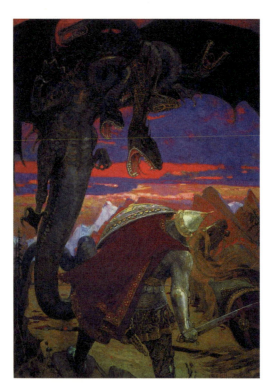

The Russian knight Dobrynya Nikitich battles a seven-headed hydra.

38

Sárkány

With its wings, its several fire-breathing heads – traditionally in multiples of three or seven – and its scales of many colours, the Hungarian dragon known as a sárkány was originally associated with the weather. Thunder and rainstorms were caused when two or more sárkány fought one other high above the clouds. Some could be ridden by humans with magical powers who were known as Garabonciás.

Once upon a time…
Historically, most stories involving Hungarian dragons cast them as villainous treasure-hoarding monsters who kidnap maidens and are slain by brave young men.

Origins:
According to some myths, a sárkány was born from a pike that had lain in mud for several months, or from a cockerel seven or 13 years old that had hidden around the house for too long.

In popular culture:
Recent Hungarian literature has reinvented the sárkány as a more sympathetic figure helping young children to develop emotionally.

Lagarfljót Worm

ccording to legends dating back to 1345, the Icelandic lake of Lagarfljót is home to a terrible serpentine creature known as the Lagarfljótsormur, or Lagarfljót Worm. Capable of crossing land and climbing trees, the beast is thought to be more than 12m (39ft) long – though some accounts suggest it is as long as the lake itself – and its appearance is said to presage some fateful event.

Once upon a time...
In the 1980s, telephone cables laid across the lake were mysteriously damaged, and the Lagarfljót Worm was blamed.

Origins:
A folktale from the mid-nineteenth century suggests that the creature was originally a slug kept by a child, which grew so large that she threw it into the lake, where it continued to grow.

In popular culture:
In 2012, a video purporting to show the worm swimming across the lake was controversially authenticated, though sceptics insisted that it merely showed a frozen fishing net caught on a rock.

The term 'worm' – or 'wyrm' in Old English – means a dragon or serpent.

"*Men really do need sea-monsters in their personal oceans.*"

– *John Steinbeck,* The Log from the Sea of Cortez

Siegfried stabs the dragon Fáfnir.

"Sleeping on a dragon's hoard with greedy, dragonish thoughts in his heart, he had become a dragon himself."

– *C.S. Lewis*, The Voyage of the Dawn Treader

Fáfnir

he dragon Fáfnir features throughout Norse mythology, including the Völsunga saga and both the prose and poetic Eddas. The possessor of a huge hoard of treasure, the dragon is ultimately slain by the hero Sigurð with the help of the sword Gram, forged by Fáfnir's brother Regin. The blood from Fáfnir's heart bestows the ability to understand birds, enabling Sigurð to anticipate Regin's treachery and kill him before he is killed himself.

Once upon a time…
Fáfnir's treasure had been given to his father Hreiðmarr by the Norse gods Odin, Loki, and Hœnir when they accidentally killed his brother Ótr.

Origins:
Before becoming a dragon, Fáfnir may originally have been a dwarf like his brother Regin. He only took on the form of a dragon after killing his father and taking his treasure.

In popular culture:
In 2015, the International Astronomical Union named a star in the Draco constellation Fáfnir, after the dwarf-turned-dragon.

The Wawel Dragon

nown in Polish as 'Smok Wawelski', the Wawel Dragon lived in a cave beneath the royal castle on Wawel Hill, demanding a weekly tribute of cattle from the people of Kraków. Unable to defeat it in battle, the king's two sons used cunning instead, feeding the dragon with cattle skins stuffed with sulphur that had been set on fire. Gulping down the skins, the beast soon burst into flames and rapidly died.

Once upon a time...
Neither of King Krak's sons would go on to inherit their father's kingdom. One son murdered the other – reports differ as to which killed which – and was exiled; their sister succeeded to the throne.

Origins:
In one version of the story, the idea of filling the cattle carcasses with sulphur came from a cobbler named Skuba.

In popular culture:
Since 1972, a statue of the Wawel Dragon has stood at the bottom of the Wawel Hill in Kraków, outside a cave believed to be the dragon's lair.

The Wawel dragon sleeps beneath the royal castle.

"Beware that, when fighting monsters, you yourself do not become a monster."

– *Friedrich Nietzsche*, Beyond Good and Evil

"I was four years old when I first met a dragon. I never told my mother. I didn't think she'd understand."

– Kelly Barnhill, When Women Were Dragons

Breathing fire, the triple-headed dragon fearlessly advances.

Kulshedra

The Kulshedra features in Albanian folklore as an enormous many-headed female dragon, sometimes disguised as a woman, salamander, frog, or turtle. Her milk is poisonous; her heads can spit fire and grow back when cut off, and she can cause any kind of natural disaster, threatening villagers with flood or famine and demanding human sacrifices. Some legends even say a Kulshedra can grow large enough to encircle the entire globe.

Once upon a time…
Many Albanian legends involve the defeat of a Kulshedra. In one, a young prince kills the dragon that has been blocking the source of a river with the help of a princess, his dog, and a horse.

Origins:
A Kulshedra is said to begin life as a snake before becoming a 'bolla', a demonic serpent whose eyes remain shut for all but one day a year, when it devours any human it sees.

In popular culture:
The Kulshedra features in an expansion of *Dungeons and Dragons*.

Leviathan

n Jewish mythology, Leviathan was a huge dragon or sea serpent – more than three hundred miles long – whose breath could boil oceans and whose eyes give forth a brilliant light. Despite his immensity, he could, however, be killed by tiny parasitic worms called 'kilbit', which would infect the monster's gills. Leviathan features six times in the Tanakh, or Hebrew Bible, and is described in the Book of Job as 'king over all the proud beasts'.

Once upon a time…
According to one legend, God originally created a male and female Leviathan, but then killed the female to stop the pair breeding and overwhelming the world.

Origins:
An earlier version of Leviathan can be found in Canaanite myth in the form of the seven-headed sea serpent Lotan, servant of the sea god Yam.

In popular culture:
Leviathan is mentioned in both Milton's epic poem *Paradise Lost* and Blake's prophetic book *Jerusalem: The Emanation of the Giant Albion*.

According to the Book of Isaiah, God will destroy Leviathan on the last day.

*"There shall be corals in your beds
There shall be serpents in your tides,
Till all our sea-faiths die."*

– *Dylan Thomas, 'Where Once The Waters Of Your Face'*

*"I am the blood of the dragon.
Do not presume to teach me lessons."*

– *George R.R. Martin*, A Dance with Dragons

A glazed brick panel from the Ishtar Gate depicts a Mušḫuššu.

Mušḫuššu

A dragon from ancient Mesopotamian mythology, the Mušḫuššu was the sacred animal of the Babylonian deity Marduk, who had defeated it and made it his servant. Its thin body was covered in scales, with front legs that resembled those of a lion and back legs like an eagle's talons. On its head stood both a crest and a pair of horns, while a snake-like tongue protruded from its mouth.

Once upon a time…
According to Mesopotamian myth, Mušḫuššu was one of 11 demons born to the elder sea-god Tiamat, who was killed by Marduk.

Origins:
The earliest known appearance of the Mušḫuššu is on a vase in the Louvre Museum, dating back to the twenty-first century BC.

In popular culture:
In the sixth century BC, the most celebrated depiction of a Mušḫuššu could be found at Babylon's magnificently decorated Ishtar Gate, parts of which can now be seen in Berlin's Pergamon Museum.

Bahram Gur and the dragon

ersian mythology tells several tales of the Shah Bahram Gur and his encounters with dragons; some of these can be found in the long epic poem *Shahnameh*, or the 'Book of Kings'. In one story, he met with a dragon while out hunting and killed it with two arrows. Cutting it open, he was shocked to discover the body of a young man inside it.

Once upon a time…
In another version of the story, Bahram Gur was hunting an ass whose foal had been eaten by the dragon; when the shah killed the dragon, the ass led him to its cave full of treasure.

Origins:
Bahram Gur, son of Yazdegerd I, succeeded his father as shah following his assassination in 420 AD.

In popular culture:
Illustrated manuscripts depicting Bahram Gur killing dragons, lions, and other, lesser creatures can be found in museums across the world.

Bahram Gur slays the dragon with his bow and arrow.

"Come not between the dragon, and his wrath."

– *William Shakespeare,* King Lear

Zilant

According to Tatar and Turkic legends, the Zilant combines a dragon's head with the body and wings of a bird and the legs of a chicken; its scaly skin and feathers are both dark grey. It once lived on Zilantaw Hill as the leader of a pack of snakes, but when the city of Kazan came to be founded there, the beast was chased away to the Kaban Lakes, where it is said to still live.

Once upon a time…
In one version of the story, the Zilant had two heads: one only ate grass, while the other devoured people.

Origins:
The name 'Zilant' derives from a Tatar word meaning 'snake', though the Tatars more commonly use the Persian word 'ajdaha' – meaning 'dragon' – to describe the monster.

In popular culture:
The Zilant was first installed as the official symbol of the Russian city of Kazan in 1730 and features prominently on the city's flag, where it is shown wearing the golden crown of Kazan.

Part-dragon and part-chicken, the Zilant was a curious creature.

"Here be dragons to be slain, here be rich rewards to gain."

– *Dorothy L. Sayers,* Catholic Tales and Christian Songs

"'You have nice manners for a thief and a liar,' said the dragon."

– *J.R.R. Tolkien*, The Hobbit

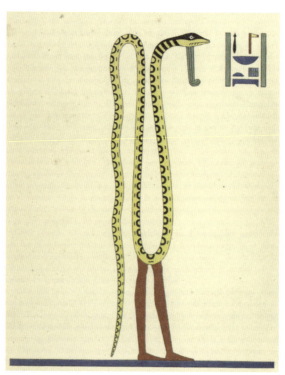

The Egyptian God Apep, depicted as a giant snake with human legs.

Apep

ften represented as a giant dragon or serpent, the Egyptian god Apep symbolised darkness and chaos. His mortal enemy was Ra, the sun god and bringer of light, and the pair would battle every night as Apep attempted to consume the sun and plunge the world into eternal darkness. To help defeat Apep, Egyptian priests and their acolytes would perform nightly rituals involving damaging wax models of the god.

Once upon a time…
Apep was said to life in wait for Ra each night as the sun god passed through the underworld in his solar boat.

Origins:
Some myths state that Apep was born at the beginning of time from the umbilical cord of his enemy Ra; others that he sprang from the spit of the goddess Neith.

In popular culture:
Apep features in the game *Assassin's Creed: Origins*, as part of the Curse of the Pharaohs expansion pack.

Ouroboros

he ancient mystical symbol of the Ouroboros depicts a dragon – or sometimes a serpent – consuming its own tail. Representing repetition, unity, eternity, and cyclical processes of destruction and rebirth, it has been adopted by a wide range of figures across history, from ancient and Renaissance alchemists to the psychologist Carl Jung, who saw it as a symbol for the assimilation of the opposite.

Once upon a time...
The serpent Jörmungandr, which encircled the world with its tail between its teeth, is a Norse version of the Ouroboros.

Origins:
Though the word Ouroboros is Greek and means 'tail-eating', the oldest known version of the Ouroboros comes from the *Enigmatic Book of the Netherworld*, an ancient Egyptian funerary text dating back to around the fourteenth century BC.

In popular culture:
In the *X-Files* episode 'Never Again', Agent Dana Scully gets a tattoo of the Ouroboros on her back.

The mystical symbol of the Ouroboros dates back to ancient Egypt.

"The baby has known the dragon intimately ever since he had an imagination. What the fairy tale provides for him is a St. George to kill the dragon."

– *G. K. Chesterton*, Tremendous Trifles

"The Ninki Nanka licks its gray-stained teeth. … It looks up at me, tongue retreating. All will die, but I will still need to eat."

– *Natasha Bowen,* Skin of the Sea

A mirror can be used to deflect the deadly gaze of the Ninki Nanka.

Ninki Nanka

 legendary black and green dragon-like creature thought to live in the swamps of West Africa, the Ninki Nanka is typically represented as combining the head of either a crocodile or horse, the neck of a giraffe, and the body of a donkey, crocodile, or hippopotamus. Not only can the beast kill with its stare, but even glancing at its body can cause the observer a dangerous illness from which few recover.

Once upon a time…
In 2006, a team from the Centre for Fortean Zoology visited the Gambia in search of the Ninki Nanka and interviewed an eyewitness who had been taken ill after watching a 15m (50ft) monster for more than an hour.

Origins:
Sightings of the Ninki Nanka were historically believed to presage catastrophes such as famines or droughts.

In popular culture:
A Ninki Nanka appears in the novel *Skin of the Sea* by Nigerian-Welsh writer Natasha Bowen.

Nyami Nyami

A dragon-like creature with the head of a fish and the body of a snake, the Nyami Nyami is thought to live in the Zambezi River with his wife; the water is said to turn red as he passes. He is worshipped by the people of the Tonga tribe who live in the Zambezi valley; they believe that he protects them and ensures that the land surrounding the river remains fertile.

Once upon a time…
The construction of the Kariba Dam in the 1950s was afflicted by several misfortunes attributed to the wrath of the beast, angered that the dam would separate him from his wife in the Kariba Gorge.

Origins:
Before the gorge was flooded, the Nyami Nyami was said to sleep under a rock known as Kariwa, 'the trap'.

In popular culture:
A sculpture of the Nyami Nyami stands to the side of the Kariba Dam wall, looking down on the lake.

Depictions of the Nyami Nyami are often carved into walking sticks in Zambia.

"'Never laugh at live dragons, Bilbo you fool!' he said to himself, and it became a favourite saying of his later, and passed into a proverb."

– *J.R.R. Tolkien*, The Hobbit

"The Sea-Dragon Kings live in resplendent underwater palaces and feed on opals and pearls."

– *Jorge Luis Borges*, The Book of Imaginary Beings

The dragon god Ryūjin is considered a patron of the Japanese people.

Ryūjin

he Japanese dragon god of the sea, Ryūjin, was a largely benevolent creature who lived in an underwater palace known as Ryūgū-jō, made of red and white coral. He could assume human shape and was able to control the tides using two magical jewels named manju and kanju: the first made the tide flow and the second made it ebb. Shrines to Ryūjin can be found across Japan.

Once upon a time…
One legend tells the story of how Ryūjin caused the jellyfish to lose its bones. The dragon needed medicine made from a monkey's liver and sent a jellyfish to bring him a monkey. But the jellyfish let the monkey escape, and Ryūjin broke all its bones as a punishment.

Origins:
Ryūjin is one of several dragons mentioned in the seventh-century Japanese chronicle *Kojiki*.

In popular culture:
In the Japanese Dragon Ball franchise, the name Ryūjin is given to a race of dragon gods.

Wani

nother type of Japanese sea dragon that features in the seventh-century Japanese chronicle *Kojiki* is the Wani, a type of shape-shifting monster that can breathe in both water and air, and – like Ryūjin – lives in coral palaces. As a sea dragon, it can control water, creating whirlpools, storms, and tidal waves, and its blessing is often sought by sailors and fishermen, fearful of its power.

Once upon a time…
According to legend, the first emperor of Japan was descended from Toyotama-hime, a shape-shifted Wani who never told her human husband of her true identity; he only discovered that she was a dragon when she was giving birth to their son.

Origins:
The Japanese characters that make up the name Wani mean 'crocodile' or 'alligator' in Chinese, and the myths surrounding the creature may derive from Chinese – or Indian – legend.

In popular culture:
Several Japanese video games feature characters similarly born to a dragon mother and a human father.

A dragon flies above the sea in this 1831 woodcut by Utagawa Kuniyoshi.

"The hunger of a dragon is slow to wake, but hard to sate."

– *Ursula Le Guin,* The Wizard of Earthsea

Zennyo Ryūō

ennyo Ryūō has been worshipped as a rain god in Japan since the early ninth century, when the country suffered a terrible drought because an abbot magically captured all the nation's dragon gods inside a water bottle. Another abbot, Kukai, prayed to Zennyo, a powerful dragon that lived in Northern India, and she came to Japan to make rain for the country before deciding to stay and live in a pond by the imperial palace.

Once upon a time…
The Buddhist priest Keien spent a thousand days living as a hermit near Mount Murō, one of Zennyo's dwelling places. A young woman asked him to teach her a charm, and when he asked her to show him her face, she revealed a dragon's claw then disappeared.

Origins:
The name Zennyo Ryūō can be translated into English as 'goodness woman dragon-king'.

In popular culture:
Zennyo Ryūō is a popular subject in Japanese art.

This painting of Zennyo Ryūō by the Japanese artist Hasegawa Tōhaku dates back to around the sixteenth century.

"The only terrifying quality that dragons do not possess is that of existence."

– *David Whiteland*, Book of Pages

"Always speak politely to an enraged dragon."

– Steven Brust, Jhereg

Japanese dragons are often associated with Buddhist monks and temples.

Kuzuryū

he Japanese dragon Kuzuryū is revered as a god with power over water, and its full name – Kuzuryū Daimyōjin – can be translated as 'Great God Nine-Headed Dragon'. Several legends about Kuzuryū tell of the dragon originally being evil – often requiring the sacrifice of maidens – before being converted to good by local Buddhist monks through prayer, preaching, or recitations of the sutra.

Once upon a time…
The annual festival at Hakone's Kuzuryū shrine commemorates a priest who prayed non-stop for three days and nights to persuade Kuzuryū to stop demanding maiden sacrifices and instead to guard the people who lived on the shores of Lake Ashi.

Origins:
Kuzuryū may have its origins in two many-headed Hindu deities, Vāsuki and Śeṣa, who are both half-human and half-serpent.

In popular culture:
Several shrines to Kuzuryū can be found across Japan; they are particularly popular with people looking for love.

Ao Guang

In Chinese legend, Ao Guang is the Dragon King of the Eastern Sea, the most powerful of the four dragon king brothers who rule the world's oceans. Able to shift between human and dragon form, he can also control the creatures of the sea, and create storms, whirlpools, and floods. He is also the owner of the Ruyi Jingu Bang, a magical weapon also used to measure the depth of the sea, until the Monkey King took it from him.

Once upon a time…
In the sixteenth-century Chinese novel *Fengshen Yanyi* ('The Investiture of the Gods'), Ao Guang fought with the young protection deity Nezha after the latter washed himself in a stream near the dragon's underwater palace.

Origins:
The four dragon kings represent the power of nature in Chinese legend.

In popular culture:
Ao Guang features in another sixteenth-century Chinese novel, *Journey to the West*, translated into English by Arthur Waley as *Monkey*, and adapted into the popular Japanese television series *Saikyu* ('Monkey').

Ao Guang struck terror into the hearts of the Chinese people.

"The dragon does not deign to crush the earthworm"

– Arthur Waley,

Monkey *(a translation of Wu Cheng'en's* Journey to the West*)*

Dragon turtle

he mythical Chinese dragon turtle combines the body of a dragon with the shell of a turtle (or, alternatively, the body of a turtle with the head of a dragon). Statues of the best-known dragon turtle Bixi – one of the nine sons of the dragon king – have adorned the funerary monuments of the country's most high-ranking figures for more than 15 centuries: one of the earliest is that of Xiao Xiu, the younger brother of the sixth-century Chinese emperor Wu.

Once upon a time…
Two of the four Chinese celestial guardians are combined in the dragon turtle: the green dragon guarding the east, and the black turtle that protects the north.

Origins:
The dragon turtle has particular significance in the Chinese art of feng shui. Placing coins near a figure of a dragon turtle is said, for instance, to result in increased wealth.

In popular culture:
In 'The Garden of Zinn', an episode of the 1980s television series *Dungeons and Dragons*, a character is bitten by a poisonous dragon turtle.

This dragon turtle statue can be found in one of the many temples in Beijing's Beihai Park.

"With money, you are a dragon; without it, a worm."

— *Chinese proverb*

"Then the storm broke, and the dragons danced."

– *George R.R. Martin*, Fire & Blood

In Chinese mythology, dragons are thought to have power over the weather, bringing storms and rain.

Shenlong

Shenlong, whose name means 'divine dragon' in English, is the Chinese dragon god who controls the wind and the rain, and who is thus revered by farmers and all those who work on the land. He is typically depicted with five claws on each foot, marking him out as one of the high-ranking imperial dragons whose image can only be used on the robes of the Chinese emperor.

Once upon a time…
The people of one remote Chinese village prayed to Shenlong to save their crops when they experienced a terrible drought. The dragon appeared to them in a thunderstorm, bringing with him much-needed rain.

Origins:
Shenlong is first mentioned in the *Shanhai jing* ('Classic of Mountains and Seas'), a Chinese text thought to date back to the fourth century BC.

In popular culture:
Shenlong features in the Dragon Ball franchise as a traditional four-clawed Chinese dragon capable of granting wishes to those who summon him.

Gaasyendietha

he dragon Gaasyendietha is said to dwell in the depths of Lake Ontario, according to the mythology of the indigenous Seneca people living south of that lake. Known as the 'meteor dragon' because it is believed to have arrived on this planet via a meteor that collided with the earth, it is said to be able to fly through the sky on a trail of fire, breathing fire of its own.

Once upon a time…
The French explorer Jacques Cartier saw a giant snake-like creature with fins swimming in the St. Lawrence River in 1534; local people told him the beast was named 'Gaasyendietha'.

Origins:
Some stories suggest that Gaasyendietha did not in fact arrive on a meteor but rather was born from the eggs of a serpent.

In popular culture:
In 1934, hoaxers attached a dragon head to a barrel filled with empty bottles and anchored it briefly in Lake Ontario; the truth was not discovered for several decades.

Lakes are popular locations for mythical beasts, from the Loch Ness monster to Lake Ontario's Gaasyendietha.

"There were dragons when I was a boy."

– *Cressida Cowell*, How to Train Your Dragon

"Even to see the Uktena asleep is death, not to the hunter himself, but to his family."

– *James Mooney*, Myths of the Cherokee

Horned serpents feature in mythologies across North America, Europe, and the Middle East.

Horned serpent

Dragon-like freshwater creatures with long teeth, horned serpents feature in the folklore of many cultures but are particularly common in Native American mythology, where they often possess the ability to control the weather and change their shape. The people of the Muscogee Creek speak of an underwater serpent with a large crystal set in its forehead, while the Potawatomi people of the Mississippi tell of a horned serpent that lived on Thunder Mountain and fought a thunderbird.

Once upon a time…
According to the Cherokee people, the horned serpent Uktena was sent to kill the sun but failed and was sent to live in the spirit world.

Origins:
Sioux legend casts horned serpents as ancient water monsters driven to extinction by thunderbirds, suggesting that the belief may have been inspired by dinosaur fossils.

In popular culture:
In the *Harry Potter* world, one of the houses at the North American Ilvermorny School of Witchcraft and Wizardry is named Horned Serpent.

Amaru

A double-headed dragon serpent, the Amaru was thought by the Incan people of South America to live at the bottom of rivers and lakes. It was associated not only with rainbows – thought to be an Amaru sucking water from one head to another – but also with revolution. Its heads may be those of a puma, condor, or llama, while its tail is typically that of a fish; its feet and wings and bird-like.

Once upon a time...
Two Amarus fought so destructively that the great creator Viracocha sent the gods of wind and lightning to put an end to their battle; their two bodies were transformed into a chain of mountains.

Origins:
Belief in the Amaru is believed to date back even to pre-Incan Andean civilizations.

In popular culture:
The association of Amaru with upheaval has led to the name being adopted by revolutionary leaders such as Tupaq Amaru II, leader of an eighteenth-century rebellion against the Spanish.

*Monsters with multiple heads – from the hydra to the Ouroboros
– are found in the mythologies of many cultures.*

"*The ant's a centaur
in his dragon world.*"

– Ezra Pound, 'The Cantos'

*"Our moon long ago, long ago
Was eaten by the bakunawa
Please have pity, return it, return it,
The crown of our king."*

– Traditional Hiligaynon song of the eclipse

A dragon and its rider cross the night sky, silhouetted against the moon.

Bakunawa

he single-horned Philippine dragon known as the Bakunawa takes its alternative name – the moon-eating dragon – from the eclipses it is believed to cause. Eighteenth-century explorers told stories of local people standing outdoors banging pans and pots during eclipses, making as much noise as possible to scare the dragon so it would spit out the moon it had swallowed. They also designed their warships to resemble the Bakunawa.

Once upon a time…
According to one Philippine myth, a tribe once burned down the house of a Bakunawa that had fallen in love with a tribeswoman. The dragon took revenge by eating the earth's seven moons, but was scared off before it could consume the last one.

Origins:
The name Bakunawa is believed to derive from two ancient words meaning 'bent snake'.

In popular culture:
A popular Philippine playground game involves one child – the Bakunawa – trying to break into a circle formed by other children to catch another child representing the moon.

Poubi Lai

 eep in the Loktak lake in Manipur, northeastern India, the evil dragon Poubi Lai once dwelled, according to the myths of the local Meitei people. Resembling an enormous python – an important spirit in Meitei folklore – it is thought to have wreaked havoc on the people of the Moirang kingdom surrounding the lake, causing death and destruction whenever it was awakened from its slumbers.

Once upon a time...
Disturbed by local fishermen, Poubi Lai demanded a daily tribute from the people of Moirang of a basket of rice and a human sacrifice. Only a shaman wielding a magical nine-pointed javelin was able to defeat the dragon.

Origins:
The shaman's javelin was magically created from an underwater plant known as a Tou.

In popular culture:
The craftsman Karam Dinesh carved a 6m (21ft) long sculpture of Poubi Lai from a single tree root in 2002. It has since been exhibited across India.

Alone on the lake, armed only with a spear, a hunter battles a dragon.

*"The fire-spewing dragon
fully had wasted
The fastness of warriors,
the water-land outward,
The manor with fire."*

– Beowulf

Dragons from Literature

Dragons have served for centuries as literary heroes' greatest adversaries. In the Old English poem *Beowulf*, the hero slays a fire-breathing dragon and is slain himself in doing so; that dragon is said to have inspired J.R.R. Tolkien to create Smaug, the fearsome foe encountered by Bilbo Baggins in *The Hobbit*. And in today's fantasy literature, dragons play prominent parts in both J.K. Rowling's *Harry Potter* series and in *A Song of Ice and Fire* by George R. R. Martin.

Beowulf stands firm against the dragon in this drawing from 1923.

Beowulf and the Dragon

In the final section of the Old English epic poem *Beowulf*, the eponymous hero – now king of the Geats – battles a dragon that has laid waste to his lands in revenge for the theft of treasure from its lair by a slave. Beowulf is mortally wounded, but his relative Wiglaf comes to his aid, stabbing the dragon with his sword so that the king can inflict the fatal blow with his dagger before he dies.

Once upon a time…
Before the dragon's awakening, Beowulf had spent 50 years as the king of the Geats after killing both the giant Grendel and his mother.

Origins:
This dragon is perhaps the earliest instance of a fire-breathing dragon in European literature; it has been linked with the biblical figures of Leviathan and the devil, and the fires of Hell.

In popular culture:
Beowulf's dragon provided J.R.R. Tolkien with the model for Smaug, the dragon in *The Hobbit*.

Beowulf uses his shield as a defence against the dragon's fiery breath.

"Then the baleful fiend its fire
belched out, and bright homes burned.
The blaze stood high
all landsfolk frighting."

– Beowulf, *translated by Francis Barton Gummere*

"My armour is like tenfold shields, my teeth are swords, my claws spears, the shock of my tail a thunderbolt, my wings a hurricane, and my breath death!"

– *J.R.R. Tolkien*, The Hobbit

Bilbo steals a golden cup from the dragon Smaug.

Smaug

maug, the principal villain in J.R.R. Tolkien's 1937 novel *The Hobbit*, is surely the most famous dragon in all English fiction. The eloquence and arrogance he displays in his long conversations with the eponymous – and invisible – hobbit Bilbo Baggins make him a deeply memorable character as well as a highly traditional adversary whose death brings the story towards its ultimate happy ending.

Once upon a time…
Smaug is eventually killed by Bard the bowman, who aims at a bare patch on the dragon's belly, its only weakness.

Origins:
Tolkien described the Old English poem *Beowulf* as one of his key sources for *The Hobbit*, and several parallels exist between that poem's dragon and Smaug: both are old and greedy, sleep atop a treasure hoard, and seek revenge for the theft of a golden cup.

In popular culture:
In the recent film versions of *The Hobbit*, Benedict Cumberbatch provided Smaug's voice.

Glaurung

Known as 'the Father of Dragons', Glaurung was the oldest of the fire-breathing dragons of Middle Earth, the setting for J.R.R. Tolkien's fantasy novels. He was created by the dark lord Morgoth to lead his forces against the elves and their allies. His magical gaze could freeze its victims in place or make them mad, causing them to forget their own identities.

Once upon a time...
Glaurung took revenge even as he was slain by Túrin Turambar: the dying dragon's blood rendered his killer unconscious and caused his sister Niënor, thinking he was dead, to drown herself in the river.

Origins:
Glaurung first appears in Tolkien's unfinished novel *The Silmarillion*, published in 1977, four years after the author's death.

In popular culture:
Glaurung appears again in another of Tolkien's unfinished works, *The Children of Húrin*, published in 2007.

Glaurung is one of four named dragons in the Middle Earth stories; the others are Smaug, Scatha, and Ancalagon the Black.

"Glaurung opened his eyes and looked upon Turambar with such malice that it smote him as a blow."

– *J.R.R. Tolkien*, The Silmarillion

Drogon, Rhaegal, and Viserion

In the *A Song of Ice and Fire* book series by George R.R. Martin, Drogon, Rhaegal, and Viserion are the three brother dragons of Daenerys Targaryen. Viserion, named after Targaryen's brother Prince Viserys, is cream coloured with golden horns and black teeth; Drogon, named after Daenerys's late husband Khal Drogo, is red and black, while Rhaegal has green and bronze scales, with yellowy-orange wings. Following the deaths of his brothers, Drogon is the last living dragon.

Once upon a time…
Killed by the Night King's spear, Viserion was resurrected to battle his brother Rhaegal, who was then shot with a scorpion bolt.

Origins:
The three dragons were born from petrified dragon eggs given to Daenerys by Magister Illyrio Mopatis at her wedding.

In popular culture:
The fantasy novel series *A Song of Ice and Fire* has given rise not only to the television series *Game of Thrones* and *House of the Dragon* but also to a card game, a board game, and several video games.

Drogon attacks some livestock in this section of the Game of Thrones *tapestry. It was inspired by the Bayeux Tapestry and is on display in Belfast, Northern Ireland.*

"If you want to conquer the world, you best have dragons."

– *George R.R. Martin,* A Dance with Dragons

"There was the Horntail, at the other end of the enclosure, crouched low over her clutch of eggs, her wings half-furled, her evil, yellow eyes upon him."

– *J. K. Rowling*, Harry Potter and the Goblet of Fire

Dragons are believed to hatch from eggs, like reptiles.

Hungarian Horntail

he Hungarian Horntail is one of many species of dragon to feature in the *Harry Potter* series of books by J. K. Rowling. With its black scales, yellow eyes, spiked tail, and sharp claws, and capable of breathing fire, the Horntail is one of the most dangerous dragons in the series, feeding on cattle, goats, sheep, and humans. The species is said to be particularly aggressive.

Once upon a time…
Harry encounters a Hungarian Horntail during the 1994 Triwizard Tournament when it is chosen as the obstacle he has to face in the Golden Egg retrieval task.

Origins:
Dragon eggs are often sold illegally in the world of Harry Potter, despite the rules of the Ministry of Magic.

In popular culture:
Hungarian Horntails have featured in the Dragon Challenge rollercoaster ride at the *Wizarding World of Harry Potter* in four Universal Studios theme parks.

The Harry Potter *books mention many types of dragon, including the Antipodean Opaleye, Chinese Fireball, and Common Welsh Green.*

"All at once there was a scraping noise and the egg split open. The baby dragon flopped on to the table. It wasn't exactly pretty; Harry thought it looked like a crumpled, black umbrella."

– *J.K. Rowling*, Harry Potter and the Philosopher's Stone

Norwegian Ridgeback

ess aggressive than the Hungarian Horntail, with browner scales and distinctive black ridges on its back, the Norwegian Ridgeback has venomous fangs and – unusually for dragons – typically eats aquatic mammals. Young Ridgebacks are born from black eggs and initially have skinny jet-black bodies with long snouts and large spiny wings; they grow quickly – trebling in length in a single week – and soon learn to breathe fire.

Once upon a time…
Norbert was a Norwegian Ridgeback secretly raised by Hagrid from an egg he'd been given by a stranger; when discovered, it was taken to live in a dragon sanctuary.

Origins:
Norwegian Ridgebacks appear in *Harry Potter and the Philosopher's Stone*, and *The Goblet of Fire*; their name is thought to be a nod towards the Rhodesian Ridgeback breed of hunting dog.

In popular culture:
In the film adaptation of *The Philosopher's Stone*, Norbert the Norwegian Ridgeback was realised digitally based on a model created by designer Paul Catling.

"Dragon blood's amazingly magical, but you wouldn't want a dragon for a pet, would you?"

– *J.K. Rowling*, Harry Potter and the Goblet of Fire

The distinctive blue flame of the Swedish Short-Snout can burn bone to ashes.

Swedish Short-Snout

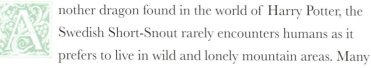nother dragon found in the world of Harry Potter, the Swedish Short-Snout rarely encounters humans as it prefers to live in wild and lonely mountain areas. Many now live in a reservation in Sweden, which forms the course of an annual broom race in which riders compete to win a trophy shaped like the dragon. The skin of the Swedish Short-Snout, covered in silvery-blue scales, is used to make protective gloves and shields.

Once upon a time…
Cedric Diggory faced a Swedish Short-Snout in the Triwizard Tournament in *Harry Potter and the Goblet of Fire*. He successfully retrieved the golden egg after distracting the dragon by transforming a rock into a dog.

Origins:
Introduced in *The Goblet of Fire*, the Short-Snout is also mentioned in *Fantastic Beasts and Where to Find Them* and *Quidditch Through the Ages*.

In popular culture:
The Swedish Short-Snout features in the game *LEGO Harry Potter: Years 1-4*, where it is one of the dragons caged by Hagrid.

Kalessin

he dragon Kalessin is the colour of iron, with long, yellow teeth and dark red wings; it appears in several of the *Earthsea* novels written by Ursula K. Le Guin. In *The Farthest Shore*, Kalessin flies Ged and Arren home after they have defeated the wizard Cob; in *Tehanu*, it burns the mage Aspen to save Ged and Tenar; and in *The Other Wind*, it helps destroy the Wall of Stone.

Once upon a time…
Tehanu, a dragon-human, is revealed to be the daughter of Kalessin at the end of the novel *Tehanu*.

Origins:
There are suggestions at certain points in the novels that Kalessin may actually be Segoy, the creator of Earthsea, who spoke the islands and light into existence, giving them their true names.

In popular culture:
The Studio Ghibli film *Tales from Earthsea*, directed by Gorō Miyazaki, is based upon elements drawn from the first four *Earthsea* novels.

Several other dragons feature in the Earthsea *novels, including Orm and his descendent Orm Embar.*

"The dragons do not dream.
They are dreams. They do not work
magic: it is their substance, their being."

– *Ursula K. Le Guin*, The Farthest Shore

Written over a period of more than forty years, the stories in the Dragonriders *series span more than two millennia.*

"My nightly craft is winged in white, a dragon of night dark sea."

– *Anne McCaffrey,* Dragonsong

The dragons of Pern

I n the *Dragonriders of Pern* series of novels by the writer Anne McCaffrey, Dragons are not mythical creatures but an alien race. Typically gold or green in colour, they broadly resemble their namesakes and are able to breathe fire by chewing a rock called firestone, which reacts with acid in one of their stomachs to produce a gas that catches fire on contact with air. They can also teleport between locations.

Once upon a time…
The only white dragon to feature in the *Dragonriders* series, Ruth was unable to break out of its egg and had to be assisted by Jaxom, whom he then bonded with.

Origins:
The Dragon race was genetically engineered by the colonist scientist Kitti Ping Yung using Pern's indigenous fire lizards to fight a destructive spore called Thread which was devastating the planet.

In popular culture:
The videogame *Dragonriders: Chronicles of Pern* for the Sega Dreamcast and PC was published in 2001 by Ubisoft.

Mythical creatures from *Legends*

Every culture has its share of fantastical mythical beasts, and the creatures in this section – ranging from powerful gods to malevolent tricksters – are drawn from Greek mythology, Celtic folklore, Norse and Hindu legend, and even the epics of ancient Mesopotamia. Not all will be familiar, and strange composites abound, like the Manticore, combining the head of a human, the body of a lion, and the tail of a scorpion ... but with two extra rows of teeth!

The god Thor battles the Midgard serpent in Henry Fuselli's painting of 1790.

Sphinx

n Greek mythology, the Sphinx was a deadly creature with the head of a woman, the body of a lion, and the wings of a bird; it asked travellers a riddle – what creature walks on four legs in the morning, two legs at noon, and three legs in the evening? – and devoured those who could not find the solution. By contrast, Egyptian sphinxes – such as the famous Great Sphinx of Giza – were typically male, benevolent, and wingless.

Once upon a time…
It was Oedipus, the future king of Thebes, who solved the riddle of the Sphinx: the answer was man, who crawls as a baby, walks upright as an adult, and walks with a stick in old age.

Origins:
According to Hesiod, the Sphinx was the offspring of the two-headed dog Orthrus.

In popular culture:
The tomb of Oscar Wilde at Père Lachaise in Paris is adorned with a sculpture of a Sphinx by Jacob Epstein.

Oedipus meets the Sphinx amidst the bodies of its victims.

"We do not feel horror because we are haunted by a sphinx, we dream a sphinx in order to explain the horror that we feel."

– *Jorge Luis Borges,* Ragnarök

"I acquired the habit of laying my egg and burning myself every five hundred years – and you know how difficult it is to break yourself of a habit."

– *E. Nesbit,* The Phoenix and the Carpet

Reborn, the phoenix rises from the flames and soars to the skies.

Phoenix

he figure of the Phoenix, the brightly coloured immortal bird who dies in fire only to rise from the ashes and be born again, is found in several mythologies, including those of the Greeks, Persians, and Egyptians. A symbol of renewal, often depicted with a halo, it has for centuries been associated with the sun and with the resurrection of Christ, and often featured in medieval European heraldry.

Once upon a time…
According to some ancient sources, a Phoenix was thought to live for around five centuries between each rebirth.

Origins:
The Greek historian Herodotus believed the Phoenix to originate from ancient Egypt; its name derives from the same root as that of the Phoenician people.

In popular culture:
In E. Nesbit's 1904 novel, *The Phoenix and the Carpet*, five children find an egg in a rolled-up carpet which hatches into a Phoenix.

Cerberus

In Greek mythology, Cerberus was the many-headed dog that guarded the gates of the underworld to ensure that the dead could never escape. With a serpent for a tail, and a body covered in snakes, this ferocious beast was typically described in literature as having three heads, though in art he has more often been depicted with two. The poets Ovid and Euphorion of Chalcis claimed that his venomous saliva poisoned the plant aconite.

Once upon a time...
The last of the 12 labours of Hercules was to capture Cerberus and bring him back from the underworld; Hercules did this with his bare hands, carrying the dog on his back.

Origins:
Cerberus was the offspring of Typhon, the serpentine giant defeated by Zeus, and Echidna, half-woman half-snake; his many siblings included the Sphinx and the Colchian dragon that guarded the Golden Fleece.

In popular culture:
Cerberus features in the animated Disney series *Hercules* as a playful and disruptive puppy.

Hercules captures Cerberus and leads him from the underworld.

*"Here Cerberus,
with triple-throated roar,
Made all the region ring."*

– *Virgil*, Aeneid

Chimera

hough its name has now come to mean any mythical creature combining parts from several other animals – or, metaphorically, an unrealistic dream – in Greek mythology the chimera was a monster with the head and body of a lion, the fire-breathing head of a goat on its back, and a snake's head at the end of its tail. In some depictions it also has the wings of a dragon.

Once upon a time…
According to Homer's *Iliad*, the Chimera was slain by the divine Corinthian hero Bellerophon on the orders of the Lycian king.

Origins:
Like Cerberus, the Chimera was the offspring of Typhon and Echidna; it took its name from the Greek word for a female goat.

In popular culture:
The names Chimera and Bellerophon both feature in the film *Mission: Impossible 2*: the former as an artificially created virus, and the latter as its antidote.

Astride the winged horse Pegasus, Bellerophon slays the Chimera.

"Chimaera ... had three heads, one of a grim-eyed lion, another of a goat, and another of a snake, a fierce dragon."

– *Hesiod*, Theogony

"'Be winged. Be the father of all flying horses,' roared Aslan in a voice that shook the ground. 'Your name is Fledge.'"

– *C. S. Lewis,* The Magician's Nephew

Bellerophon captures Pegasus using the golden bridle given to him by Athena.

Pegasus

he winged horse Pegasus is one of the most recognizable creatures in Greek mythology. The bearer of the sky god Zeus's thunderbolts, he lived in the stables on the divine Mount Olympus and was rewarded for his service by being turned into a constellation. His hooves were said to create magical springs whenever they touched the ground, including those on Mount Helicon and Pirene in Corinth.

Once upon a time…
In some versions of the story of Bellerophon and the Chimera, the hero was assisted by Pegasus, who had been caught with the aid of a golden bridle provided by the goddess Athena.

Origins:
According to legend, Pegasus and his human brother Chrysaor were born when the blood of the gorgon Medusa, killed by Perseus, landed on the earth.

In popular culture:
Pegasus features prominently in the stop-motion animated film *Clash of the Titans*, rescued by Perseus from the monstrous Calibos.

Centaur

With the upper body of a human and the legs and lower body of a horse, the centaurs found in Greek mythology were wild, barbaric creatures, often drunk, who lived in the mountains of Thessaly and Arcadia. They were descended from Ixion and the cloud nymph Nephele – according to some accounts, via their son Centaurus and the mares of Magnesia. The best-known centaur, Chiron, was more civilized and served as tutor to the demigod Asclepius.

Once upon a time...
Centaurs attempted to abduct Hippodamia on the day of her wedding to Pirithous, king of the Lapiths, and were only defeated when Pirithous's friend Theseus joined the battle.

Origins:
The myth of the half-human half-horse centaur is thought to have originated when men on horseback were encountered by people from cultures with no concept of riding.

In popular culture:
In the *Chronicles of Narnia* by C.S. Lewis, centaurs are wise, brave, and noble creatures, fighting alongside Aslan against the White Witch, and acting as healers and astronomers.

The zodiac sign of Sagittarius is typically represented as a centaur armed with bow and arrow.

"It is a most special and unheard-of honour to be allowed to ride a centaur. I don't know that I ever heard of anyone doing it before."

– *C.S. Lewis,* The Silver Chair

"Draw very close to Scylla's cliff and drive thy ship past quickly; for it is better far to mourn six comrades in thy ship than all together."

— *Homer*, Odyssey

As Odysseus's ship passes Scylla, several crewmen
are lost to the many-headed monster.

Scylla and Charybdis

According to Greek myth, two sea monsters lived on opposite sides of the Strait of Messina. Scylla, on the Calabrian side, ate men that came near her, while Charybdis – on the Sicilian side – created whirlpools that could pull ships underwater. Sailors attempting to pass through the strait would face a difficult choice, since avoiding one of the monsters would inevitably result in encountering the other.

Once upon a time…
In the *Odyssey*, Odysseus followed Circe's advice and sailed closer to Scylla than Charybdis, losing several sailors to the man-eating monster, but avoiding his ship being swallowed by a whirlpool.

Origins:
In one story, the goddess Amphitrite poisoned the well that the nymph Scylla drank from, turning her into a monster; Charybdis, the daughter of Poseidon, was punished by Zeus for helping her father steal land.

In popular culture:
The expression 'Between Scylla and Charybdis' means being forced to choose between two equally dangerous options.

The Cyclopes

A race of one-eyed giants, the Cyclopes of Greek mythology form three distinct groups. The first, mentioned in Hesiod's *Theogony*, are the three sons of Uranus and Gaia, who gave Zeus the thunderbolt they had created in return for freeing them. The second group are the primitive shepherds encountered by Odysseus in Homer's *Odyssey*. The third and final group are the powerful builders who constructed the walls at Mycenae, Tiryns, and Argos.

Once upon a time…
Odysseus and his men were captured – and some of them eaten – by the Cyclops Polyphemus. The remainder escaped, tied to the bellies of the giant's sheep, after the wily hero plied his captor with wine and then blinded him with a stake.

Origins:
The Greek name Cyclopes – Cyclops is the singular form – means 'round eyes'.

In popular culture:
In Marvel's *Avengers*, Cyclops is a mutant who can fire powerful energy beams from his eyes.

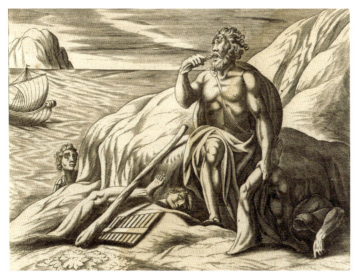

The cyclops Polyphemus chews on a bone as Odysseus's ship approaches.

"We Cyclopes do not fear Zeus or any other god, for we are stronger by far than they are."

– *Homer*, Odyssey

"Long indeed is the story of Perseus and the Gorgon Medusa."

– *Pindar,* Nemean Odes

In some versions of the myth, the Gorgons had wings – as well as snakes – on their heads.

Gorgons

hree terrifying sisters with poisonous snakes for hair and the ability to turn anyone who looked at them to stone, the Gorgons – Sthenno, Euryale, and Medusa – lived at the edge of the world, beyond the river Oceanus. Of the three, only Medusa was mortal, and she was beheaded by Perseus, who used a mirrored shield to look at the Gorgon without being turned to stone.

Once upon a time…
Perseus sought divine help to slay Medusa: Hephaestus provided a sword, Hades a helmet of invisibility, Hermes winged sandals, and Athena a mirrored shield.

Origins:
According to the poet Ovid, Medusa was a beautiful young woman assaulted by the sea god Neptune and then transformed into a monster by the goddess Athene.

In popular culture:
A 2008 sculpture by the Argentinian artist Luciano Garbati, *Medusa with the Head of Perseus*, inverts the myth, depicting the Gorgon as victorious.

Griffin

The majestic Griffin, combining the head, wings, and talons of an eagle with the body of a lion, can be found in a wide range of mythologies across Europe and Asia. Often associated in classical times with the gods Apollo, Dionysus, and Nemesis, it gained new religious connotations in medieval Europe, where its double nature made it a potent symbol for Christ, simultaneously human and divine.

Once upon a time…
In Dante's *Divine Comedy*, the Griffin draws the chariot bearing Beatrice and refuses to eat from the tree of knowledge.

Origins:
The earliest depictions of Griffins date back five millennia or more and can be found in ancient Egypt, where they were associated with the falcon-headed sun god Horus.

In popular culture:
Images of Griffins have been used as part of the logos of several businesses including the Midland Bank, Vauxhall Motors, and the United Paper Mills.

This engraving of a griffin is by the fifteenth-century German artist Martin Schongauer.

"Blessed art thou, O Griffin, who dost not Pluck with thy beak these branches sweet to taste, Since appetite by this was turned to evil."

– *Dante*, The Divine Comedy

"There do the hideous Harpies make their nests, Who chased the Trojans from the Strophades, With sad announcement of impending doom."

– *Dante,* The Divine Comedy

In Act III of Shakespeare's play The Tempest, *the spirit Ariel takes the form of a harpy during a banquet scene.*

Harpy

alf-human and half-bird, harpies were believed by the ancient Greeks to be the agents of Zeus, delivering offenders to their punishment; later sources cast them as guardians of the underworld. Always depicted as vicious, violent, and hungry, harpies are sometimes represented as beautiful and other times as monstrously ugly: the Greek poet Hesiod mentions their 'lovely hair', while the tragedian Aeschylus, writing two centuries later, describes them as disgusting.

Once upon a time…
Blinded after angering Zeus, King Phineus of Thrace was tortured by the harpies, who prevented him from eating. He was rescued by Jason and the Argonauts, who drove off the harpies in return for directions.

Origins:
Harpies were originally believed to be spirits of the winds, snatching away people and possessions.

In popular culture:
'Harpy' has been a term of abuse for uncompliant women since at least the time of Shakespeare, who has Benedick refer to Beatrice by the term in *Much Ado About Nothing*.

Minotaur

The legendary Minotaur – a beast with the head of a bull and the body of a man – lived in Knossos, Crete, in a labyrinth designed, on the orders of King Minos, by the architect Daedalus and his ill-fated son Icarus. Every nine years, the Athenians would send seven young men and seven young women to Crete to be devoured by this terrible monster.

Once upon a time...
The Minotaur was ultimately slain by Theseus, who used a thread given to him by Minos's daughter Ariadne to find his way around the labyrinth.

Origins:
Medieval and Renaissance versions of the Minotaur sometimes depict a beast with the head of a man and the body of a bull.

In popular culture:
Versions of the Minotaur have appeared several times in the television series *Doctor Who*. One story, 'The Horns of Nimon', features a race of bull-headed aliens – the Nimon – who receive regular tributes of young people from the planet Aneth.

In some versions of the story, Theseus kills the Minotaur by stabbing it in the throat with his sword.

"*Every labyrinth has its minotaur.*"

– *Carlos Ruiz Zafón,* The Angel's Game

Unicorn

ypically depicted as a white horse with a single long horn on its forehead, the unicorn dates back four millennia. The ancient Greeks believed it to be real, and in Renaissance times it was seen as a symbol of purity. Its horn was said to protect those who drank from it from both poison and epilepsy, and consequently, Narwhal tusks were often sold to unsuspecting buyers as unicorn horns.

Once upon a time…
Marco Polo wrote of having encountered unicorns in Sumatra, describing them as being similar in size to elephants, with a single black horn in the middle of their foreheads. It seems likely that he confused a unicorn with a rhinoceros.

Origins:
A version of the unicorn somewhat resembling a cow appears on Bronze Age stamp seals found in the Indus valley.

In popular culture:
The unicorn is the national animal of Scotland. Long associated with rainbows, it has in recent years also become a symbol of the queer community.

Woven in the Netherlands at the turn of the fifteenth century, the seven medieval tapestries known as The Unicorn Tapestries *were rediscovered in the 1850s.*

"Well, now that we have seen each other," said the unicorn, "if you'll believe in me, I'll believe in you."

– *Lewis Carroll,* Through the Looking-Glass and What Alice Found There

"'Goodness gracious me!' exclaimed the Faun."

– *C.S. Lewis,* The Lion, the Witch and the Wardrobe

Though fauns and satyrs resemble each other physically, fauns are typically shy while satyrs are often drunk and boisterous.

Faun

epicted since Renaissance times as creatures with the head and upper body of a human and the horns, legs, and tail of a goat, Fauns have typically been seen as cheerful, good-natured creatures who play flutes and other musical instruments. Though sometimes foolish, they are usually friendly towards the humans who stumble across them in the lonely woodland places they call home.

Once upon a time...
The original Fauns were woodland spirits,
followers of the Roman forest god Faunus.

Origins:
As Faunus increasingly became identified with
the Greek god Pan, so his followers the Fauns
came to resemble satyrs, half man and half goat.

In popular culture:
Probably the best-known Faun of all is Mr
Tumnus in C.S. Lewis's novel *The Lion, The Witch
and the Wardrobe*. Lewis stated that the whole
idea for the novel came to him from the mental
image of a faun carrying parcels and an umbrella
through a snowy wood.

*"Then, water-kelpies haunt the foord
By your direction
An' nighted trav'llers are allur'd
To their destruction."*

– Robert Burns, 'Address to the Deil'

A kelpie returns to the waters as the sun begins to set.

Kelpie

In Scottish folklore, a kelpie is a beautiful but dangerous horse-like water spirit which can at times adopt a human form. Some kelpies were said to lure humans to their deaths by appearing in their equine form already saddled and bridled and seemingly ready to be ridden; when mounted, however, they would immediately rush towards the nearest river or loch to drown their rider.

Once upon a time…
A kelpie captured by the Laird of Morphie and forced to help build his castle is said to have cursed the laird's family, causing their destruction.

Origins:
The first written mention of kelpies appears in an eighteenth-century ode by the poet William Collins, published in 1788.

In popular culture:
Since 2013, a pair of hundred-foot-high sculptures of kelpies designed by Andy Scott have stood outside Falkirk in Scotland, where the Forth and Clyde Canal meets the River Carron.

Selkie

agical shapeshifting creatures found in Norse and Celtic mythology, selkies can take the form of either seals or humans. Their sealskin plays a vital role in their transformation between forms: they shed the skin to adopt a human shape and must place it back upon their shoulders to return to seal form; stealing a selkie's skin traps it in its human existence.

Once upon a time...
In a story from the Scottish islands, a woman who fell in love with a selkie gave birth to a son with the face of a seal.

Origins:
Though selkies feature in the mythologies of many cultures, their name is Scottish and comes from the Scots word for seal.

In popular culture:
The 1994 film *The Secret of Roan Inish*, written and directed by American auteur John Sayles, tells the story of a young girl exploring her family's mysterious relationship with selkies.

Separated from its sealskin, a selkie is trapped in human form.

"It was a while ago, in the days when they used to tell stories about creatures called the Selkie Folk."

– *Mollie Hunter*, A Stranger Came Ashore

Dwarf

hort-statured, mountain-dwelling, bearded craftsmen with a taste for ale, dwarves are some of the most familiar figures in European folklore, appearing in many myths and literary works, from the medieval *Nibelungenlied* – in which a dwarf called Alberich is described as having the strength of seven men – to the novels of J.R.R. Tolkien, where a band of dwarves accompany the hobbit Bilbo Baggins on a quest to defeat the dragon Smaug.

Once upon a time…
In the Old Norse poem 'Alvíssmál', a dwarf asks to marry Thor's daughter, but the god delays him by asking him questions, until the sun comes up and turns the dwarf to stone.

Origins:
The plural spelling 'dwarves' originates with J.R.R. Tolkien, who admitted in 1937 that his use of the term was 'just a piece of private bad grammar'.

In popular culture:
The 1937 Walt Disney film, *Snow White and the Seven Dwarfs*, gave the eponymous dwarfs their individual names, which were chosen from a shortlist of more than 50.

In Arthur Rackham's illustration from Wagner's Das Rheingold, *Alberich whips his miserable dwarf subjects.*

*"The dwarves of yore made mighty spells,
While hammers fell like ringing bells
In places deep, where dark things sleep,
In hallows halls beneath the fells."*

— *J.R.R. Tolkien,* The Hobbit

Elf

riginally tiny and mischievous sprites akin to fairies, who might steal away children before their christenings, fire their characteristic elf-bolts at cattle, or give sleepers bad dreams by sitting on their chests, elves have increasingly been identified as beautiful, magical, and noble creatures, similar in size to humans. This new type of elf is particularly popular in fantasy fiction and role-playing games such as *Dungeons and Dragons*.

Once upon a time...
In the medieval ballad *Lady Isabel and the Elf Knight*, a noblewoman elopes with an elven knight who then explains that he intends to kill her. Putting him to sleep with a charm, she kills him with his own dagger and escapes.

Origins:
The name 'elf' comes from old Germanic terms for evil spirits which are associated with the colour white and with beauty.

In popular culture:
The film *Elf*, starring Will Ferrell as a human raised by Santa's elves, reflects a long association between elves and Christmas, dating back to the mid-nineteenth century.

*An elf polishes his sword in this painting
by the Swedish artist Johan August Malmström.*

*"Mount off, mount off, thy lily-white steed,
And deliver it unto me
For six pretty maidens I have drowned here
And the seventh thou shalt be."*

– Lady Isabel and the Elf-Knight

> *"I am dead to all the world ...
> I am the monster that breathing men
> would kill. I am Dracula."*
>
> – *Bram Stoker,* Dracula

*The Hungarian-American actor Bela Lugosi played Dracula
many times, both on stage and on screen.*

Vampire

tories of vampires – undead creatures who consume human blood – can be found in a great many cultures, dating back several millennia, from the demons of ancient Mesopotamia to the twenty-first-century *Twilight* series by Stephenie Meyer. In most mythologies, vampires – being already partly dead – can only be slain through special methods: these can include driving a stake through the heart, decapitation, or the burning of the vampire's corpse.

Once upon a time…
In 1725, the Serbian peasant Petar Blagojević was said to have murdered his son and drunk his blood – several days after his own death and burial…

Origins:
Most of our contemporary vampire myths are associated with central Europe, and particularly Transylvania, now part of modern Romania.

In popular culture:
Vampires became a popular subject for fiction in the nineteenth century, with John Polidori's 1819 novel *The Vampire* leading a trend taken up by Joseph Sheridan Le Fanu's *Carmilla* and Bram Stoker's *Dracula*.

Jörmungandr

In Norse mythology, the sea serpent Jörmungandr, also known as Miðgarðsormr, is said to be so huge that it can encircle the entire earth by biting its own tail. When the serpent lets go of its tail, according to the thirteenth-century text *Gylfaginning*, it will result in the flooding of the seas, and the movement of the beast onto the land, signalling the coming of Ragnarök: the destruction and rebirth of the world.

Once upon a time…
Myths tell of the Norse god Thor once going fishing with a giant, and catching Jörmungandr with his line, before the giant cut the serpent free.

Origins:
Jörmungandr only grew to his giant size after Odin threw him out of Asgard – home of the gods – and into the ocean.

In popular culture:
The Midgard Serpent is a Marvel comics character based on Jörmungandr; he battles Thor – a superhero version of the Norse deity – in several encounters over more than 50 years.

This depiction of the Midgard Serpent about to take Thor's bait is from a seventeenth-century Icelandic manuscript.

"This serpent grew so greatly that he lies in the midst of the ocean encompassing all the land, and bites upon his own tail."

– *Snorri Sturluson,* Gylfaginning

Vritra

he serpent Vritra, a demon whose name means 'obstacle' or 'the enveloper', is the personification of drought in Hindu mythology. According to one story, the demon was summoned into existence by his father Tvashta to avenge Indra's killing of his other son Vishwarupa, but Tvashta's mispronunciation of the creation spell meant that Vritra would not slay Indra but would instead be slain by him.

Once upon a time...
Vritra kept the world's water captive, causing a terrible drought. Indra, the king of the Hindu gods – and also the god of war, rain, and wind – killed Vritra with a thunderbolt, releasing the water for the monsoon rains.

Origins:
The story of Indra's defeat of Vritra appears in many places, including the Rig Veda, one of the four sacred Hindu texts.

In popular culture:
Indra's defeat of Vritra serves as a symbol of the victory of good over evil and order over chaos.

Vritra was defeated by Indra, the Hindu god of the weather.

"Like arrows released in the four directions, the demon's body grew, day after day."

– *Veda Vyasa*, Srimad Bhagavatam

"My brother believed in all sorts of mythical creatures: pixies, dragons, werewolves, honest men."

– *Jodi Picoult*, The Storyteller

Varuna, the Hindu god of the sky, oceans, and water, is often depicted riding on the back of a Makara.

152

Makara

In Hindu mythology, the Makara is a sea creature ridden by Ganga, the goddess of purification and forgiveness, and of the Ganges river. It is typically depicted as combining the front half of a land animal – often an antelope or elephant – with the back half of an aquatic creature such as a fish, seal, or dolphin; it has also been identified with the several types of crocodile, the water monitor, and the Gangetic dolphin.

Once upon a time…
When villagers feared that their fishing boats would be sunk by sea monsters, they would seek protection from the Makara, carving symbols of the creatures on their boats.

Origins:
The name 'Makara' means 'water monster' in Sanskrit; the Hindi word for crocodile, 'magar', derives from the Makara.

In popular culture:
Images of Makara are a common motif in Hindu temples, often adorning the structural supports either side of archways.

Manticore

With the head of a human (but with three rows of teeth in its mouth), the body of a lion, and the tail of a scorpion, the manticore may have originated in ancient Persian myth, but it became a common feature in the medieval European bestiaries that compiled descriptions and illustrations of real and what have turned out to be imaginary animals. In some depictions, manticores had spines on their tails that they could shoot like arrows.

Once upon a time…
The ancient Greek physician and historian Ctesias claimed to have seen a manticore that had been brought from India and given as a present to the Persian king.

Origins:
The name 'manticore' derives from two Old Persian words meaning 'man' and 'eat', marking the creature as a man-eating monster.

In popular culture:
In *Dungeons and Dragons*, manticores can speak and often attempt to humiliate their opponents by getting them to beg for their lives.

This illustration of a Manticore comes from the thirteenth-century Rochester Bestiary, held in the British Library.

"The Manticore prefers to eat humans; it will slaughter many, lying in wait not for single men but for two or even three at a time."

– *Claudius Aelianus,* On the Characteristics of Animals

Mermaid

With the head and torso of a woman and the tail of a fish, mermaids are common figures throughout the world's mythologies, often falling in love – either happily or tragically – with human men. In 1493, the explorer Christopher Columbus reported seeing mermaids in the Caribbean, reporting that they were 'not half as beautiful as they are painted', but it is thought that what he saw were manatees, which would explain his disappointment.

Once upon a time…
In Hans Christian Andersen's fairytale *The Little Mermaid*, the heroine falls in love with a human prince but is doomed to die unless she kills him.

Origins:
One of the earliest stories of hybrid fish/human creatures tells of Oannes, a Mesopotamian figure who was said to have the body of a fish but with a human head and feet beneath his fish's head and tail.

In popular culture:
A Disney film of Andersen's fairytale was released in 1989, removing many of the story's darker elements.

A mermaid draws a crowd of fish astonished at her beauty.

"*Her skin was so clear and shrewd as a rose petal, her eyes were as blue as the deepest lake, but like all the others she had no feet; her body ended in a fish's tail.*"

– *Hans Christian Andersen*, The Little Mermaid

"One evening before the night prayer the rabbi forgot to remove the seal from the Golem's mouth, and it flew into a rage, rushing through the streets in the darkness, smashing everything in its way."

– *Gustav Meyrink,* The Golem

The word 'truth' is written on a Golem's head to bring it to life.

Golem

n Jewish myth, golems are silent humanoid servants created from clay which come to life when letters from the Hebrew alphabet are placed in their mouths or on their foreheads; when the letters are removed, they are deactivated. (In some versions of the myth, the letters must spell the word 'truth' in Hebrew; erasing one letter changes the word to 'death'.) Golems were thought to protect the Jews from persecution but could also be overly literal in their interpretation of their instructions.

Once upon a time…
The sixteenth-century rabbi Judah Loew ben Bezalel was said to have created a golem to protect the people of Prague, carefully deactivating it every Friday so it would rest on the Sabbath. One Friday he forgot, however, and it killed several people.

Origins:
According to the *Talmud*, Adam was first created by God as a golem before becoming a man.

In popular culture:
Between 1915 and 1920, the German director Paul Wegener made three silent horror films based on Gustav Meyrink's 1915 novel *The Golem*. Only one survives.

Picture Credits

Alamy: 11 (Masterpics), 22 (Iconographic Archive), 26 (imageBROKER), 29 (The Picture Art Collection), 30 (The Granger Collection), 33 (Ivy Close Images), 42 (AF Fotografie), 49 (Chroma Collection), 56 (Gado Images), 80 (Steve Lillie), 88 (Ivy Close Images), 97 (Associated Press), 108 (Realy Easy Star), 115 (Science History Images), 117 (David Keith Jones), 118 (Ian Dagnall Computing), 121 (The Granger Collection), 122 & 125 (Chronicle), 133 (Ivy Close Images), 135 (Everett Collection Historical), 136 (Album), 138 (Dusan Kostic), 143 (Lebrecht Music & Arts), 146 (World History Archive), 149 (Science History Images), 152 (The Protected Art Archive), 155 (The History Collection), 157 (Pictorial Press), 158 (Steve Lillie)

Amber Books: 15, 64, 76, 92, 98, 100, 151

Dreamstime: 55 (Momcilojovanov), 75 (Fredericaraujo), 83 (Tanaphong Sattayamit), 112 (Enea Kelo), 141 (Lcrms7)

Getty Images: 8 (Heritage Images), 91 (Transcendental Graphics), 130 (Culture Club), 145 (Heritage Images)

Metropolitan Museum of Art, New York: 34, 53, 111, 129

Lucy Pitts: 19

Public Domain: 16, 38, 67, 69, 73

Shutterstock: 12 (Dream Expander Studio), 21, 25, 37, 41, 45 (DeepGreen), 46, 50 (Storm Is Me), 59 (Elina Zoidberg), 60, 63 (Matthew Wesley Miller), 70, 79, 84, 87, 95, 102, 105, 106, 126 (Natalia Tan)

Decorative alphabet Paseven via Shutterstock
Background illustrations AprintStore, Natalia Barashkova, BigJoy, LeoTroyanski all via Shutterstock